This igloo book
belongs to:

....

iglöobooks

Published in 2015
by Igloo Books Ltd
Cottage Farm
Sywell
NN6 0BJ
www.igloobooks.com

LEO002 0615
2 4 6 8 10 9 7 5 3
ISBN 978-1-78440-333-1

Printed and manufactured in China

SHREK

DREAMWORKS

igloobooks

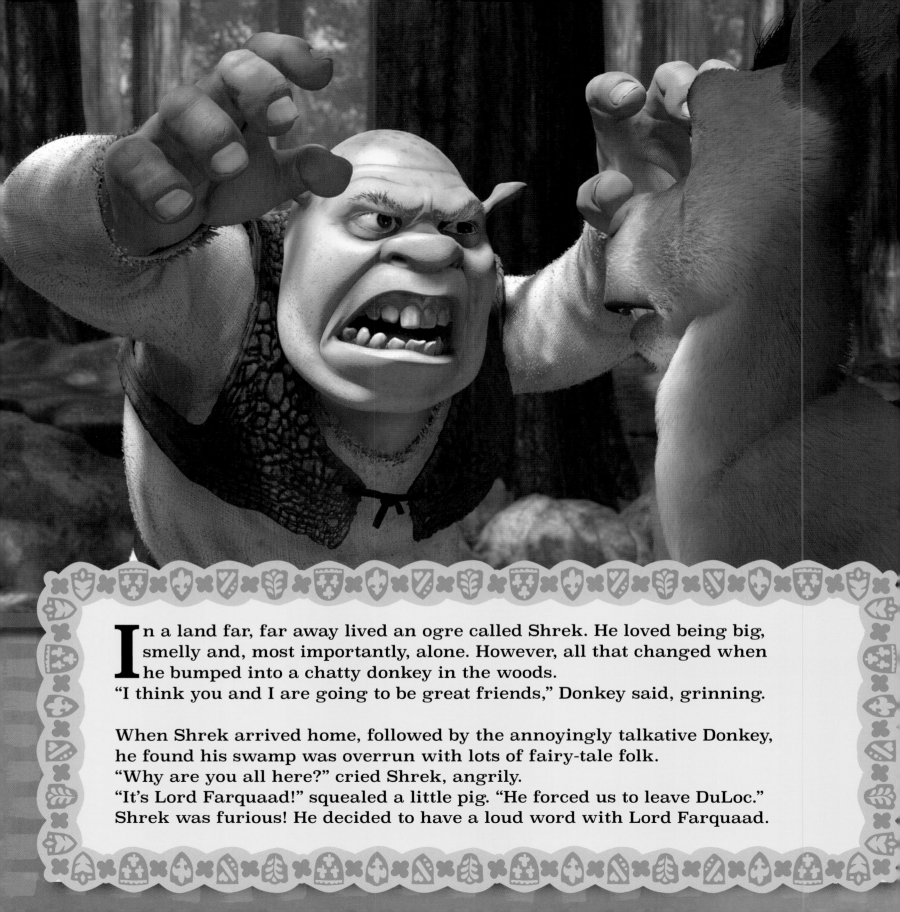

In a land far, far away lived an ogre called Shrek. He loved being big, smelly and, most importantly, alone. However, all that changed when he bumped into a chatty donkey in the woods.

"I think you and I are going to be great friends," Donkey said, grinning.

When Shrek arrived home, followed by the annoyingly talkative Donkey, he found his swamp was overrun with lots of fairy-tale folk.

"Why are you all here?" cried Shrek, angrily.

"It's Lord Farquaad!" squealed a little pig. "He forced us to leave DuLoc."

Shrek was furious! He decided to have a loud word with Lord Farquaad.

Meanwhile in DuLoc, Lord Farquaad was talking to his Magic Mirror.
"Mirror, mirror, on the wall, is this not the most perfect kingdom of them all?"
The Magic Mirror reflected. "It cannot truly be a kingdom for it has no king," it said.
Then, the Mirror showed Farquaad three princesses and explained that, by marrying one, he would become the King of DuLoc.

Farquaad chose a beautiful princess named Fiona, but there was a dragon guarding her.
"Hmm," schemed the cowardly Lord Farquaad. "I'll hold a tournament and the champion will win the 'honour' of rescuing her for me!"

Shrek and Donkey arrived in DuLoc just as the tournament was beginning in the stadium.

As Shrek walked in, Farquaad thought up a new plan.
"He who kills the ogre will be named champion," he announced. Knights charged Shrek. His only choice was to fight. The crowd gasped as he knocked down every knight, one after the other.

"Congratulations, Ogre," said Farquaad. "You've won the honour of embarking on a great quest."
Shrek just wanted his swamp back.
"I'll make you a deal," said Farquaad. "Rescue Princess Fiona and I'll return your swamp." Shrek agreed.

Shrek grabbed a suit of armour and the two friends left DuLoc.
"I don't get it, Shrek," said Donkey. "Why didn't you pull some of that
ogre stuff? You know, grind Farquaad's bones to make your bread."
"There's a lot more to ogres than people think," answered Shrek. "Ogres are
like onions. They both have layers."

Before long, the flowery fields of DuLoc gave way to a barren wasteland
of dark jagged rocks and a pungent odour filled the air.
"It's brimstone," said Shrek. "We must be getting close to the dragon."

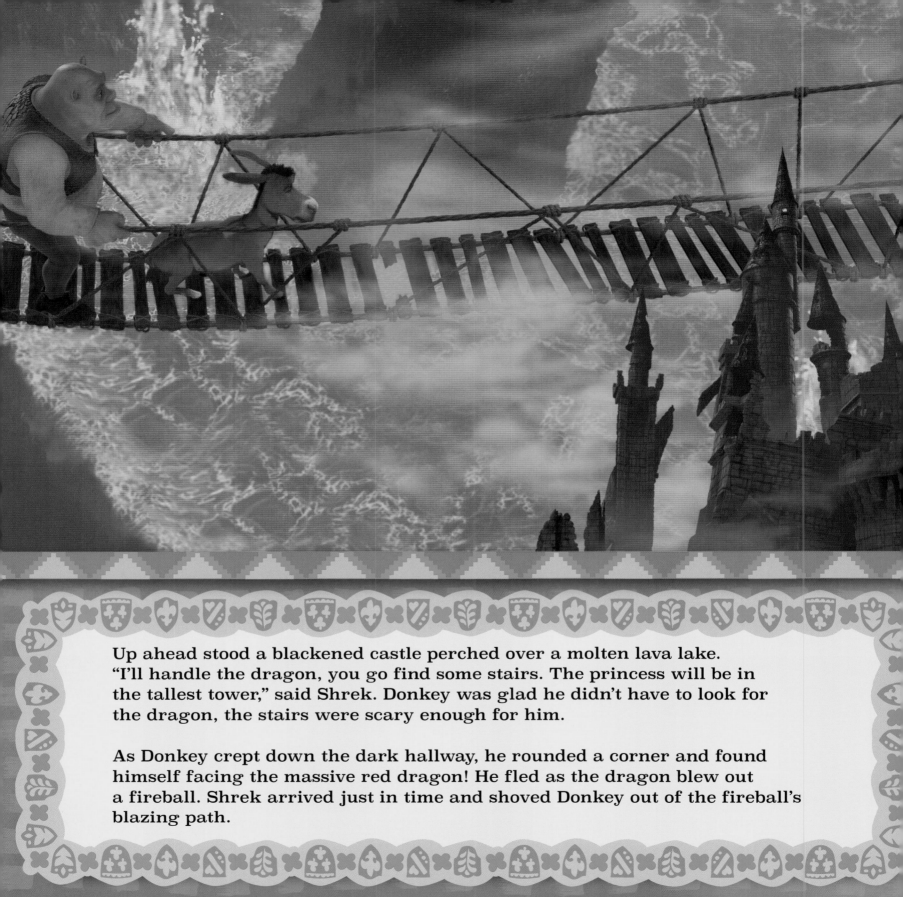

Up ahead stood a blackened castle perched over a molten lava lake.
"I'll handle the dragon, you go find some stairs. The princess will be in
the tallest tower," said Shrek. Donkey was glad he didn't have to look for
the dragon, the stairs were scary enough for him.

As Donkey crept down the dark hallway, he rounded a corner and found
himself facing the massive red dragon! He fled as the dragon blew out
a fireball. Shrek arrived just in time and shoved Donkey out of the fireball's
blazing path.

Shrek grabbed the dragon's tail, but it sent him flying high
into the sky and towards the tallest tower. He crash-landed in Princess Fiona's bedchamber.

"Are you Princess Fiona?" asked Shrek.
"I am," she said. "Awaiting a knight as bold as you to rescue me."
"Let's go," he said abruptly.
"Wait," pleaded Fiona. "Should our first meeting not be a romantic moment?"

It was clear the princess thought the armour-clad mystery man was her handsome prince.
"No time," said Shrek, grabbing Fiona by the arm.

Meanwhile, Donkey decided to do what he did best - talk.
"What large white teeth you have," he chattered. The dragon batted its
eyelashes and Donkey realised it was a girl dragon. He'd flirt his way
out of danger!

Just as the dragon pursed her lips for a kiss, Shrek swung on a nearby chain
and tried to grab Donkey. THWUMP! Shrek missed. He let go of the chain and
the end of it came crashing down, landing like a collar around the dragon's
huge neck. Shrek, Donkey, and Fiona ran.

Safely away from danger, Fiona turned to Shrek.
"You rescued me!" she cried. Her fairy-tale was finally coming true.

Now it was time for the kiss she'd been waiting for. Fiona demanded
that Shrek remove his helmet. As he did, she just stared.
"You're… an ogre?" she asked.
"I was sent to rescue you by Lord Farquaad. He wants to marry you,"
explained Shrek.
"Well, then tell him to rescue me!" she snapped.
"I'm a delivery boy, not a messenger boy," said Shrek,
as he flung Fiona over his shoulder.

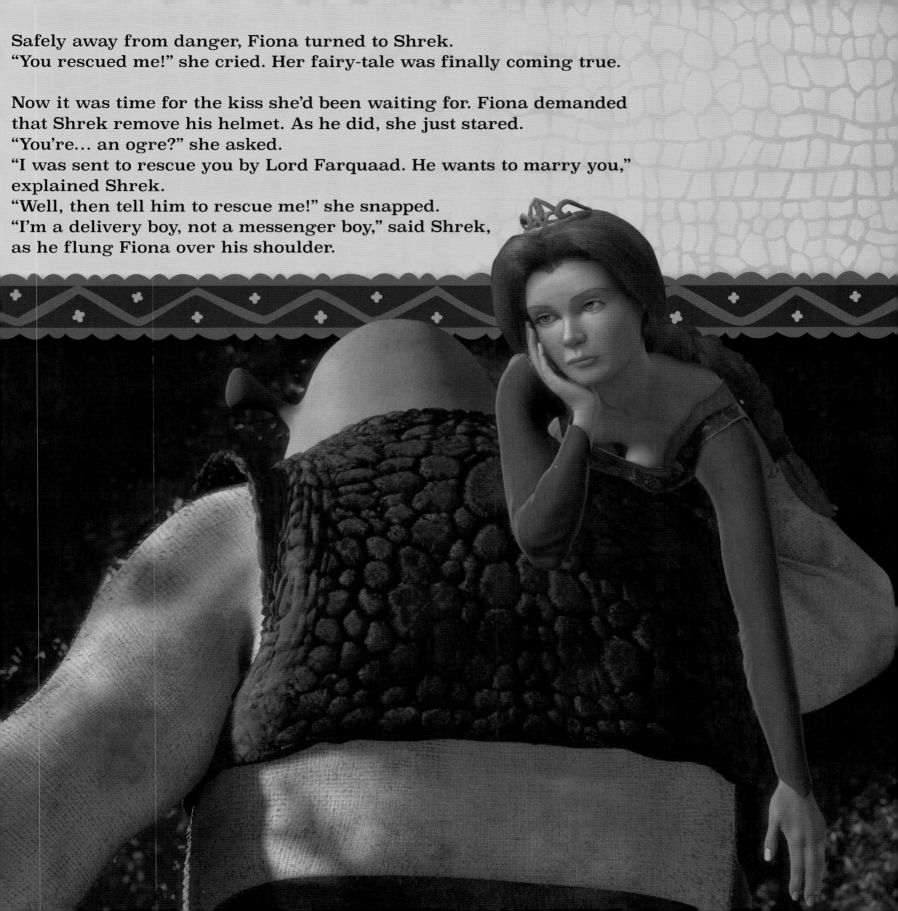

Shrek was determined to deliver Farquaad's bride as soon as possible and get back to his swamp, so he walked and walked and walked without a rest.

As Fiona talked with Donkey, she looked up at the fading sun. "Shouldn't we stop to make camp?" she asked, nervously. Shrek ignored her, but suddenly he was interrupted by a voice that seemed too loud and large for a princess. "I need to find somewhere to camp now!" Fiona demanded.

As they settled down, gazing at the night stars, Fiona hid herself in a nearby cave just before the sun disappeared.

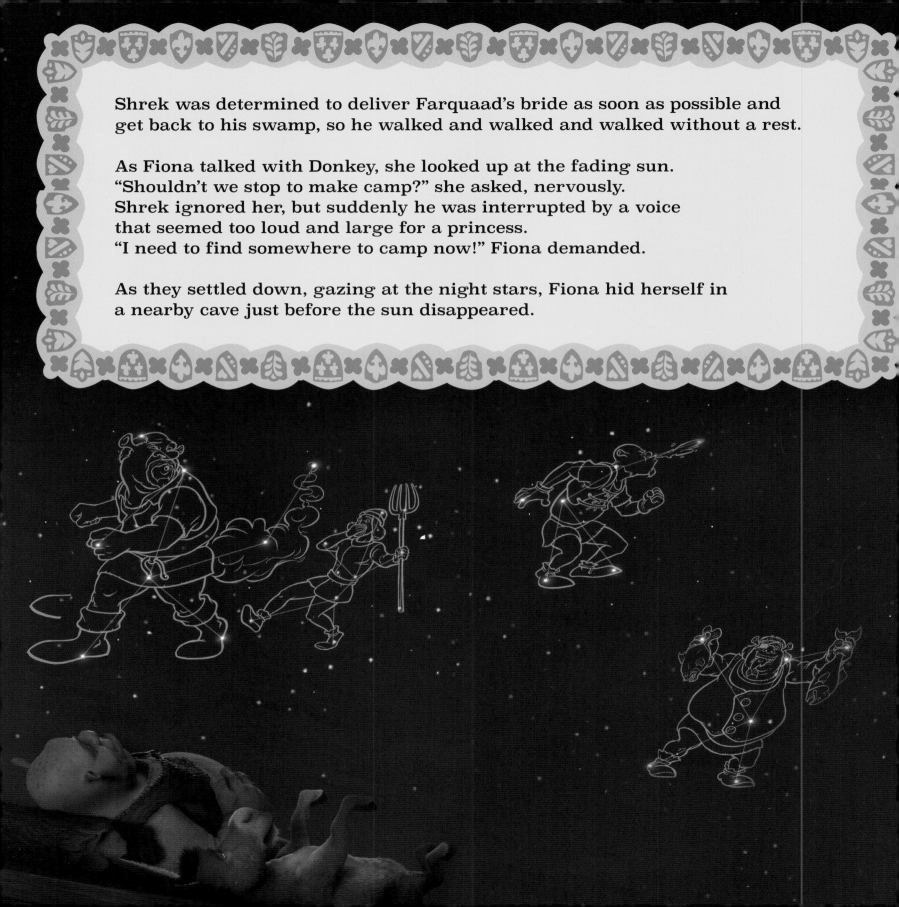

In the morning the trio set off again. They hadn't been walking long when
a man in green leaped from a branch and swept Fiona into a tree.
"I'm Robin Hood and I'm rescuing you from this green beast," he declared.
He jumped to the ground and called his Merry Men. Shrek was outnumbered.

"Hiyaaaah!" Fiona leaped into action. Within minutes, she had knocked out
Robin and all of his men. Shrek and Donkey looked on, stunned and amazed
at the princess' outburst.

As they began to continue on their journey, Donkey noticed that Shrek had been shot with one of Robin Hood's arrows. "Shrek's hurt!" panicked Donkey. "He's going to die."

Fiona remained calm and removed the arrow carefully. After that, Fiona and Shrek spent the rest of the day doing nice things for each other. Fiona whipped up a cotton-candy-like treat made of cobwebs and bugs for Shrek and he returned her gift with one of his own, a frog he inflated into a balloon. They were having so much fun together that they were no longer in a hurry to see Lord Farquaad.

That afternoon, they made camp by an old mill and Shrek cooked up
his speciality, weedrat.
"Ummm, delicious," said Fiona, wolfing it down.
The princess and ogre gazed at each other.
"Isn't this romantic?" Donkey interrupted. "Just look at that sunset."
Fiona looked up, said a quick goodnight and raced into the mill.

"I know you two were digging each other," said Donkey to Shrek. "Just go
tell her how you feel."
"There's nothing to tell," said Shrek. "She's a princess and I'm an ogre."

Donkey crept into the mill to talk to Fiona, but was surprised to see an ogress!
"It's me!" hushed Fiona. "A witch cast a spell on me. Every night I become this
horrible beast. That's why I have to marry Farquaad. Only true love's first
kiss can break the spell."
"What if you married Shrek, instead?" suggested Donkey.
"Look at me, Donkey," she said.

At that moment, Shrek approached the mill door.
"Who could ever love a beast so hideous and ugly?"
Shrek thought she was talking about him and walked away, sadly.

The next morning, Shrek stomped up to Princess Fiona.
"I've bought you a little something," he sneered. It was Lord Farquaad
and his army! Shrek snatched the deed to his swamp and stormed off.
"Princess," said Farquaad. "Will you be the perfect bride for the perfect groom?"

Fiona shot an angry glance at Shrek. "Let's get married today, Farquaad,"
she said, faking a smile. Farquaad agreed.

He and Fiona rode off together and Donkey, with an anxious last look at Fiona,
hurried after Shrek.

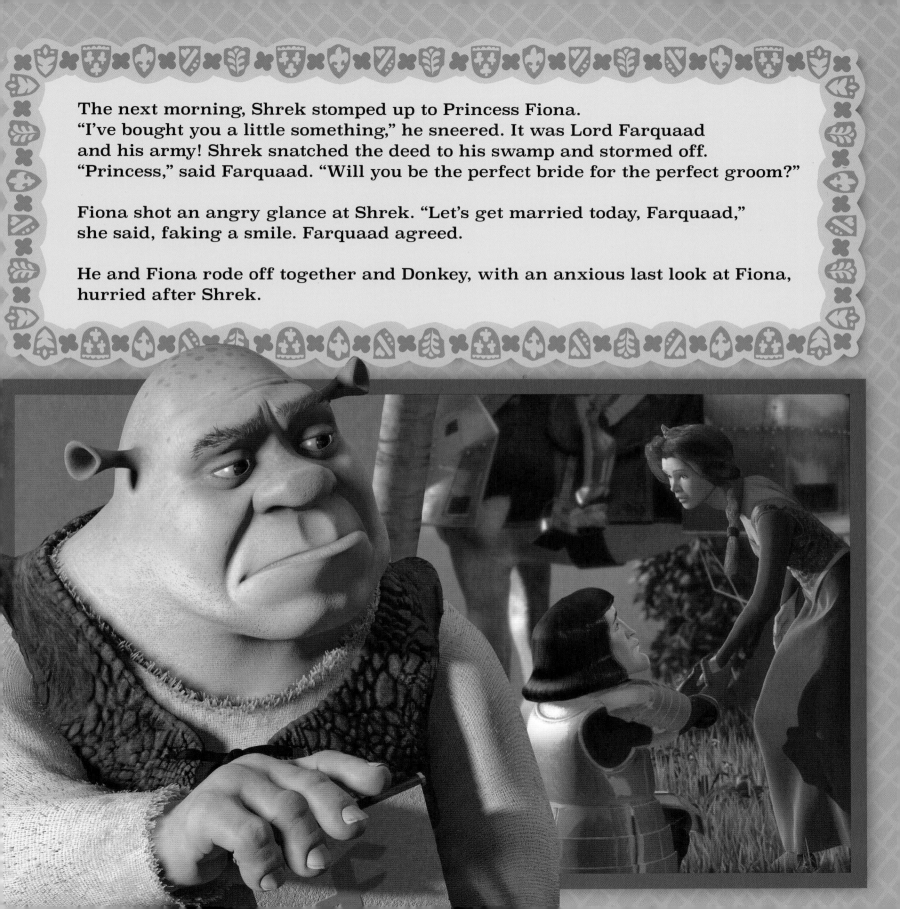

Back home at the swamp, Donkey was talking to Shrek.
"You're afraid of your own feelings, onion boy," said Donkey. "All Fiona ever did was like you.
Maybe even love you."
"She said I was ugly!" replied Shrek.
"What? When. In the mill? She wasn't talking about you!" cried Donkey.

Shrek realised he had made a mistake. "I have to stop the wedding, Donkey!" he cried..
Donkey whistled and Dragon swooped in.
"We've er… stayed in touch," said Donkey, smiling. "I guess it's
just my animal magnetism."

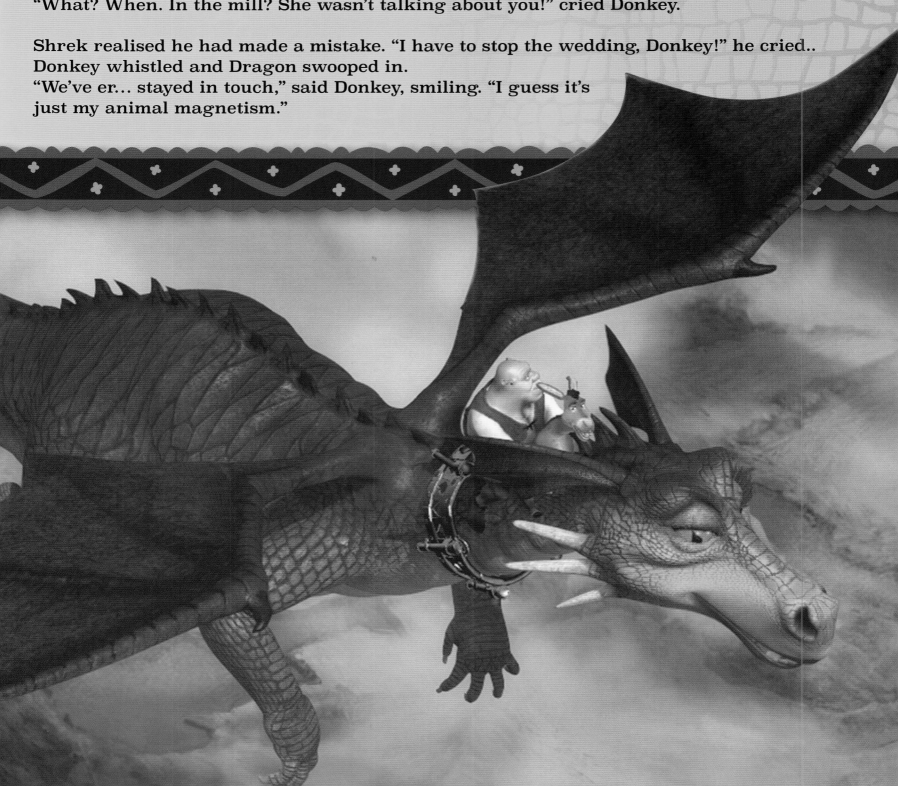

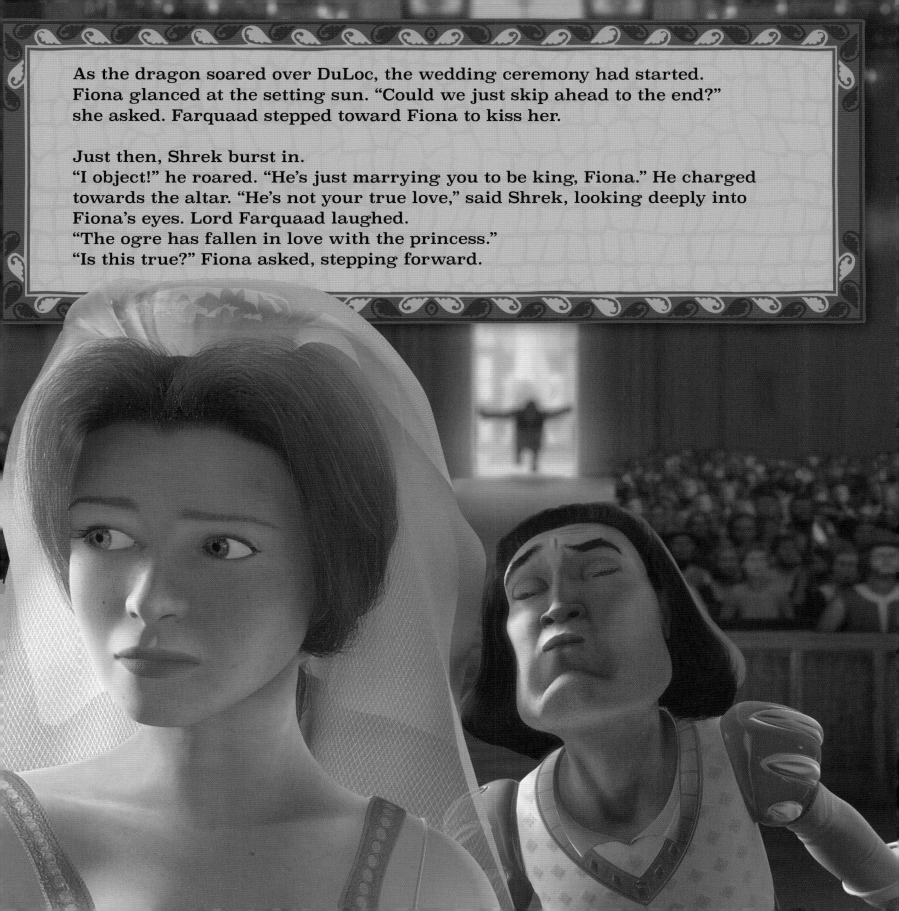

As the dragon soared over DuLoc, the wedding ceremony had started.
Fiona glanced at the setting sun. "Could we just skip ahead to the end?"
she asked. Farquaad stepped toward Fiona to kiss her.

Just then, Shrek burst in.
"I object!" he roared. "He's just marrying you to be king, Fiona." He charged
towards the altar. "He's not your true love," said Shrek, looking deeply into
Fiona's eyes. Lord Farquaad laughed.
"The ogre has fallen in love with the princess."
"Is this true?" Fiona asked, stepping forward.

At that moment, the sun set behind a hill and Fiona transformed into a plump, green ogress. Farquaad was horrified.

"That explains it," said Shrek. "Why we have so much in common."

"I'm still king," cried Farquaad, ordering his knights to kill the ogre.

Farquaad grabbed Fiona. "As for you, you will be locked up in the tower for the rest of your life." Just as Farquaad's men surrounded Shrek and his friends, he gave a piercing whistle and Dragon crashed in, swallowing Farquaad in one gulp.

Shrek turned to the princess.
"Fiona," he said. "I love you."
"I love you, too," Fiona replied. They kissed and the ogress floated into the air
and was shrouded in flashing light.

Finally, Fiona fell to the floor. The crowd waited in suspense to discover what
love's true form would be. When Fiona rose again, she was still an ogress.
"I don't understand. I'm supposed to be beautiful."
"You look beautiful to me," said Shrek. "Marry me?"
"Yes!" cried Fiona.
And they lived together, happily ever after.